Cryptic Dreams in Verses

Chapbook I

Berserker Lotus™

This is a work of fiction, and the views expressed herein are the sole responsibility of the author. Likewise, certain characters, places, and incidents are the product of the author's imagination, and any resemblance to actual persons, living or dead, or actual events or locales is entirely coincidental.

Book design by *Aesthetic Adeel*

Published by Berserker Lotus™, 2025

Printed in the United States of America

ISBN: 979-8-218-72305-7 (paperback)

e-mail: illusinblue@hotmail.com

Author's Note

If I were to tell you that this would be your typical poetry book, I would be lying. I decided to journey down a different path to writing poetry. Many of these poems originate from my nightly dreams, which I transformed into poetic language. Each poem has its own story that connects with surreal aspects of a dreamlike world and is layered in a way that is meant to be sequential. However, none of these poems were meant to be related to one another, since the dreams they are derived from possess a different string of events. Along the way, you might find a similar overarching theme as you read its contents, following the trail of significance from one to the next. These dream verses will tap into the subconscious mind, offering insight into the world the soul experiences during a deep slumber, and will make you wonder if we are merely sleeping at night.

Disclaimer

This book contains language and descriptions of suicidal ideation, depression, and anxiety. It is not intended to glamorize, glorify, or discriminate. Please read at your discretion. If you, or someone you know struggles with suicidal ideation, anxiety, or depression, please seek help from a mental health professional.

Dragon Source

Eons ago, I was frozen in an ice chamber
a block of ice upon a towering glacier.
My form was a solid speck, blemishing the sleek, pristine ice
as if a painter dripped a droplet of irregular paint from a paintbrush
onto the canvas--a canvas of crystal blue glass.

Heat rose from the edge of the ocean,
melting the ice in slow motion.
The sun beamed as bright as a thousand stars.
A thunderous roar sounded from above, where an astounding
heavenly dragon flew in a boundless frenzy.

Its scales were salmon orange from nose to tail,
with a soft, white underbelly and a masculine
head encased within its jaws. With a mighty charge
through the gusts of wind, the dragon took straight flight
towards me like an unstoppable arrow on a fierce course to its end-
where I was its only target.

Mid-flight, the dragon came to a dead stop;
its talons gripped tightly around my neck,
and its claws pierced the ice. From its steaming breath,
fuming against the ice, omniscient words spawned
from its gaping jaws: "Do not forget me."

Its fiery breath liquified the ice, awakening me
from the imprisonment of a comatose state.
Like a heavy acorn, dropping from the branch of a tree,
I descended and sank into the ocean. No longer conjoined
to the ice glacier, I was free all the while sinking
into the oceanic waters of the deep, blue sea.

The waters were unable to contain me.
As if I were spat out like a spoiled piece of fruit,
my body sprouted to the surface, with my head floating
above the waves. A spring-greeting smile widened across my face.
Thick, dark curls covered my head, and caramel-brown skin
coated my entire child-like vessel.

Cherries dangled from the cross-hatched crown
of twigs wrapped around the top of my head.
Wisdom beyond ancient years was tangled
into the narrating words the dragon spoke:
"Before the land was created,
I created the waters and the sky."

Like a loving father, the dragon swept down under me,
sliding me down on top of its back to secure me amid
flight into the atmosphere. I perched myself up like a proud
Queen, holding my position as the dragon came to a standstill.
Miles beneath me, two creatures were warring with each other,
fighting to overpower and dominate the other.

One of the creatures was a hybrid between a giant
caterpillar and a grizzly bear, while the other was
a polar bear. Natural form versus abnormal fusion.
Claws and teeth clashed. Blood splattered across
the snow, and the ferocious growling waged on.

Illumination dawned upon me, bearing me the fruit
of its secrets. The warring onslaught between
the two creatures symbolized climate change
and nature trying to reclaim its rightful place
for balance through the changing seasons.
Sun and moon switched places, round and round
like a merry-go-round, every time blood was drawn.

Axquan the Shapeshifter

Dancing in the ballroom, everyone tapping their shoes.
My eyes look up at the chandeliers. An ancient gaze
I recognize from a past life. The crooked crow of a man
slips through the crowd of tuxedos and twirling gowns.

A shapeshifter he was--a possessor of many forms.
Contact of living flesh with his would merge the two
into one ghastly beast. Mutated shape now spoke from
the lips of a new vehicle. Priestesses in disguise magnified
their protection over me. Closer and closer the gap between
us shortened as was his time in the body not of his own.

Flash of golden pupils piercing me like snake eyes.
His hand reached out to grab me. I barely escape
from his desperate grasp. An eternal waltz seeking
to conceal my existence. Like ripples in the water
and like dominoes that fall one by one from an outside
force, the shapeshifter synced, merged, and possessed
every male dancer in the room who lost their ego
to his cause to capture me until he could reach
my presence again.

His new form graced him with charm and chivalry.
I found myself entranced in the softness of his hands
cupping mine in the warmth of a miniature sunbathed cave.
Sharp teeth glistened in the deceiving smile he wore.
A ploy was being born in the scheming mind of his
that endlessly designed labyrinth upon labyrinth of devised
schemes that persisted in evolution and reproduction like cells
forming new cells at an infinite rate. I saw no bounds
to the lengths he was willing to go to play his tricks.

Was he going to reveal the Joker card from his sleeve
and give himself away as though he were a black speck
on pearly whites, or a stain of Merlot wine on sheep wool?
Now that he finally had me in his greedy hands, he could
easily hypnotize me as if I were a newborn babe enthralled
by the simplest instruments of rattling and dangling decorations.

Silence stills the room with a shivering chill.
Lips of the villain raise and lower, opening a
pandora's box, bending and shifting reality
upon the words spoken. "Ive come to kiss
your delicate hand to gain the powers
you possess. Otherwise, perhaps
I could sever your hand if you decide
to resist me. I came a long way and
followed you through lifetime after lifetime.
You might remember the one we shared
together in the ancient time of the Aztecs."

Recollection of his previous form struck a chord.
Before he could speak another word, I severed
his head with an axe. His head rolled on
the glassy, polished-white floor like a marble.
What I thought was over only continued
as words miraculously spewed from
his mouth only for the purpose of
sharing his name…………..
…….Axquan.

Lover of the Aztec Warrior

Darkness shrouded over me
Silent like a cemetery in the night
A sparkling green amulet swung side
To side from a long chain pinched
Between shriveled fingertips
Of a soothsayer

Bold dark hair and desert tan skin
Of an Aztec man appeared
Centuries from the ancient Aztec
Past was where he originated
Words from the soothsayer
Resurrected a forgotten
Memory, "He was once you and
You were once him."

Vivid recollections painted a
Vibrant scene of indigo mountains,
Purple skies, and dancing flames
Motionless with an intense focus
The other half of my existence
Living in the Aztec warrior
Bore his eyes into mine

We were left completely bare
With no clothing to shield
The naked flesh
Hoarse voice following strict
Demands barked from a distance
Domineering mother of a woman
Gaves us the order to
Initiate the ritual

Fellow tribe members crowded
Like lurching branches
To watch for their own
Amusement and curiosity
Sharp steel from the
Edge of the blade glided
Down the slopes of my palm
Leaving little streams
Of crimson

I allowed my fingers
To be a guiding instrument
Painting strange symbols on his
Forehead and collarbone as
If he were merely a canvas
To explore my creative technique
Blood with the smell of iron
Sealed our bond
He accepted it as a badge of
Honor
He and I were now one

Jealous members of the tribe
Trapped him in a dark cave
Clairvoyance and an invisible
Thread through fused blood
Created a link and bestowed
The sight to see
His tragic fate

Ferocity consumed the band
Of men who slammed heavy
Rocks and sticks on his head
Like he was a crooked
Nail on a wooden frame
Needing to be hammered down

The blood of my sacred love
Leaked from his skull
His soul essence abandoned
The vigorous warrior's body
Imprinted on from birth
To his untimely death
Now forgotten and
Discarded like a pair of
Worn out shoes

Like a wilting flower
His body slumped
To the ground
Overwhelming darkness
Swamped and filled
Every edge and crevice
Of the cave

Revelations of Deceit

Determined, misplaced, extraordinary wolf-maiden hovers
Leering at a dirt mound in the forest
She plunges her fist down into the soil
For what she hears is prickly crawling
Weaving through roots and Rocks alike—*hideous!*

A centipede, long and black with thousands of legs
In one tug she lifts it up from the ground
Like pulling out a loose shoe lace
With vigor she chomps it down, gnawing at the
Tough shell enclosing its squishy, gritty insides

Malice consumed her and she ripped it in two
To end its misery as it no longer
Served a purpose other than being recycle
Waste for the regrowth of lilies and daffodils, or roses

Mysterious girl spots this vagabond maiden out of
Thousands and countless of other distinct
Wooded settings, yet here she discovers
A hybrid creature to whom she could share
Delicate piece of gossip ears might yearn for
To remedy the itching desire of revealing
Secrets to those who are completely oblivious
Like a serpent bearing gifts of knowledge
She whispers into the maiden's ear shocking
Revelations that illuminate true colors of fellow
Maidens who were once believed to be sisters

Pink balloons shrouded her vision of her sisters'

Cackling with vile ambition to tear her asunder
Absolute avoidance seized her as she closed
The school locker so she could banish the vision
From her memory even though her efforts were futile

Left with no other option, the mystery girl grabbed
A pair of rose-colored glasses from the
Hollow hole in the tree and gently placed it
In the maiden's soft hands as if they were
Precious pearls from another dimension passed
Down like an heirloom through many generations
To now serving as a magical artifact
That bestows the wearer an ability
To see true intentions

Scientists Preying Upon Dreams

Ominous fluorescent light banishes the haze
From my mind as I witness
Scientists with white lab coats
Tinkering, meddling, prying and undressing dreams
One notices eyes peering from the
Corner zone line within the cubic
Prison where I was beseeched to
Offer powerful foresight for their advanced
Mission to find a hidden power
Possessing unimaginable, divine, supernatural
Prowess no soul could confine in one single
Infinite existence defined by the boundaries
Of space like a million sandboxes
containing reality times reality squared
Without any spared lines
And this was exactly, undoubtedly
Why the vultures in lab coats truly
Desired to possess this power

The scientist fired up the gadgets
Like Christmas lights to project an
Electronic display tying into the dimensional
Field that might capture a distinct
Resonance before nightfall, leading them to
The dream mine of divine powers
The entire island was floating in
The aqua sky attached to a
Goddess's head rising upward like a
Monument with dyed hair-a pink
Mane of unbridled color

A porcelain Goddess's visage
Majestically sculpted from the structure
In the middle of the trail
Some miles away from the base
Of the smooth, glossy neck of
The bright pink-haired Goddess was
An enlightened fountain enclosed by a
Circular, ringlike formation of white stones
Resonating, rioting, and pulsing, creating ripples
A scrying reflective color pierced through
My mind's eye, revealing the location
Of my long-lost power

Birds took flight, directing my vision
To the right chamber, where it was
Secured by the stone walls of abandoned sites
None of the calculated, dedicated scientists
Had any previous knowledge that my
Powers were what they strived
Searching for all these decades
By the time one of the Scientists
Noticed my peculiar behavior,
They ignited an ability to manifest
A psychic jellyfish to interact with my field
All nine tentacles from the pink
Jellyfish behind their head reached to
Contact my outer field, but instantly failed

Vibrant glow emanated from the blue
Violet jellyfish as it repelled the
Scientist's attempt to steal the secrets
Writhing within my third eye
Echoing, dry, humdrum voices sounded from
The tile-paved hallway, repeating the
Lone, idle word, "dreams", like a

Broken, mindless A.I.
Hundreds of men in desireless,
Black suits saunter in a single-file line
Following a villainous, cruel mastermind
Who wishes to steal people's fire-lit dreams

Until I could find them,
They all continued to mindlessly
Tread down the ill-fated path
While reciting their one-track song
Silent now their voices went, as
I sensed time slipping away
From my grasp
In an enclosed cage, slightly sectioned
Off from the other mind-control labs
The sinister experimenter smiled
A crooked smile, as he shined
A piercing white light upon piles
Of tools for torture and prying
Open a human brain

His ripened victim sat down in
An unsightly grey chair without an
Obvious frightened expression
Eyes glanced upward, forces
Siphoning the life from them
Fingers gliding along the gleaming silver
Torture items on display as if carefully
Deciding how to acutely and gracefully
Dissect a unique specimen
Under selective, precise vision
A cone-shaped, slender spear-like
Tool with a pointed kind of edge
Was chosen
Lodged by the tip of the spear

Invitingly puncturing the upper and middle eye
Where the epicenter of dreams lies

17

Wizard of Arcane Sorcery

Old, haggard wizard with a scraggly
grey beard, pointed hat, and plain
black drapes sheathing his feeble
body sowed his delicate, malicious
influence into the crawlspaces of a hero's mind.
The wizard mustered his ambitious plot
and tricked the young hero by simply
pointing toward the darkest opening
into the depths of the ominous cave
with the crooked-bone finger lined
up to the path to follow as he sweetened
his deceptive words like sugar cane,
promising a glorious prize at the edge
of the void.

Absent-minded and intoxicated by the
persuasive, hypnotic words, the young,
undefeated hero wandered into the
perilous cave without second-guessing
the reasoning behind his steps. Through
the darkness of the void and beyond
the edge of the rocky ridges of the
cave's esophagus, dwelled two ancient,
mystical entities that stood against time
and possessed the very essence that could
determine and alter one's fate.

A tall, cloaked figure--some kind
of hybrid creature with a sharp
skeletal beak of a pelican--crouched

over a boxing ring from a protruding
stone perch. Standing firmly in the
center of the ring was a monstrous
yeti with a broad-shouldered constitution
and husky proportion. Like a marionette,
the young hero was guided into the ring
by the wizard who placed him under
a plaguing spell. Cowardice ambition
thwarted the wizard and swallowed
his sound mind into madness, reeling
his decision to turn the wheel into
his favor of capturing the ancient
spellbooks at any cost.

Even if it meant casting a human
pawn into the void to do his bidding
without ever suffering a single injury.
Upon entering the ring, the young hero
challenges the yeti only to have his
feeble attempts of being an honorable
champion in combat squandered. One
fell swoop, he collapsed to the ground,
being knocked on the side of his head
with a clobbering, hairy-knuckle fist.
Once was not enough to satisfy the
Gods of the ring, even as the young
hero was already sorely defeated
and knocked unconscious. For mere
amusement, the pelican-skull creature
manipulated time to repeat the event,
rewinding to the moment when the
young hero steps into the ring.

Hope sparked the hero's courage
once more that he might escape

and triumph with his strength
and dignity intact. Yet, he was
none the wiser that this was an
effortless trick these Gods have
mastered years before his ancestors
were even born. It was only a tease
to make him think he had an advantage
to correct his last fighting strategy.
Endlessly, like swatting a fly, the yeti
wailed and smashed its fists into the
hero until it was the pelican's turn
to rewind time to restart the beating
process all over again. No soul ever
witnessed the wizard obtaining the
spellbooks, or the hero leaving with
his life spared. Unaware of the ordeal
her lover was suffering, a lady of pristine
youth and unyielding beauty spent
her days in oblivion, picking daisies
for the couples being courted in the arena.

Mother of a Serpent and a Spell of Old

Groaning in the pains of labor
Bellowing out to the stars above
Gracious divine beauty in all favor
Of the Goddess, giantess, mother of love
Swollen with pregnancy, bursting with blood
Crown of starlight floats upon her head
German stone homes beneath her feet
Feel rough to the touch

A snake weaves in and around the
Womb with its tail piercing through
Like a needle and thread
Villagers scream and scamper
With faces of dread
Minds swirl in a maddening
Whirlwind of fear causing a
Cannibalistic frenzy

Whispers of stolen spells spread
Astronauts with pink mohawks
Chase the purple-cloaked lady
Risky it was to blindly believe
She was the one who stole
Stole from a cursed town of old
That would cast a thousand year
Devastation and leave a heavy toll

Daughter of the White Anaconda

Coiled snake around the tree
glory in white; a giant anaconda.
Purple and serene its eyes gleamed.
Roots of the tree spread through the ground.
A family tree, or tree of life it seemed.
The father snake spoke to me.
From father to daughter, I discovered
I was its spawn. Proof of lineage
was traced along the freckles of my arm
that shaped the Draco constellation.
With the tip of his finger, an older man
revealed this bloodline secret, filling me
with fascination. Merely by using my arm
as a road map.

At any time, if in need, I could
call upon thee. For power, guidance,
or protection from the madness on
this planet. Ripe with pregnancy,
a radiant woman was awaiting
the birth of her newborn. Her grace
and beauty were akin to a swan.
Bronze hair glistened like wheat
in the sunlight upon her head.
Gold freckles beaming from the
roots of her angelic brunette hair.
Pulses rippled and echoed inside
the dome of her womb. A new babe
wrestling and playing in its unpredictable
setting, accepting its fate.
Birth could not be escaped.

New landscape of possibilities
to be explored. Summoning of fairies
was a necessity to protect and shield
the mother and her babe from worldly
dangers. Spring, pastel-colored fairies
sparkled in their flight. Raindrops of
honeydew sprinkled from their wings,
manifesting sporadic dust of glitter.
Every step I took, the fairies followed
in perfect harmony. Traveling in a horde
of miniature magnitude. In unison,
the fairies and I healed and shielded
the mother in loving service and gratitude.

Witch Hunter and the Enchanted Runes

Sleek, black-robed maiden
mother of a son with rosy
cheeks of which she gave him.
Sheltered by a stone cottage
on a farm, far away from any carnage.
An unknown disease tortured
the frail child known as Gabriel.
Daunting hours were spent
searching and experimenting
like a woman in labor, desperate
to birth a cure for a child so
innocent and pure.

His mother, cloaked in her
witch robe, carved and created
runes, using stones while her
precious Gabriel with golden
hair like sheep wool laid in
his crib, oblivious to ungodly
sins that deserve such punishment.
How could anything in his
unadulterated existence permit
this kind of suffering? Transfixed
upon the herbs and potions, on
the wooden counter, his mother
pondered. In a forsaken language,
she chanted spells, causing a green
glow to flash from the rune-engraved
stones.

Unbeknownst to her, another

witch was seeking to destroy
this power and her son along
with it, traveling from town-
to-town. A life-threatening
knock pounded at the door-
a knocking that was unwelcome
and one that the mother never
heard before. Pounding on the
wood, sending splinters of fear,
pricking at the mother's mind.
Rain poured down from the sky,
barely touching the witch-hunter's
eyes, cloaked by the dark, over-
shadowing hood. Without an answer,
the witch-hunter tiringly stood.

Only a candlelight flickered
by the glass window. Its warmth
detached from the outside realm
of which the witch-hunter remained
until someone or something confirmed
her suspicion. Paying no mind to
the outside world, the maiden-mother-
witch casted a spell she spent her well
of time and youth to finish so her precious
Gabriel could heal. Yet, beyond the cottage,
she and her son, Gabriel, had lived and bonded;
from nuzzling to coddling, she knew not
what lied in wait in that outside realm.

Resting Place Among the Stars

Blood spilled like wine
Under the Twilight stars
Of the midnight sky
Swordsmen wielding lances
fought in a calamitous war
from opposing sides of the field

My son Gabriel led his Knights
In arms from the front of the charge
Caution was abandoned
Steel, cold armor, and chainmail
Clashed with arms thrashing
And blades plunging into
Deep masses of flesh
Bursting guts and bodies
Crashing upon heap piles
Of the dead

Gabriel fell on his head
Resting on my lap till
He drew his last breath
His Knights in arms
Aimed their lances
At the stars, performing
A funeral ritual
By the tip of my finger
Pointing upward like
An arrow of a compass
His soul traveled in pursuit
Of the constellation

Of where he belonged
In the cluster of starry
Dust flared like the
Shape of a scar painted
Over with a gunk
Mixed in pink and white

Raptured from the Underworld

Silence deafens and suffocates
the once lively room, enclosing
everything within a tiny black hole.
Following an unrecognizable
shadow, I find myself stepping
on cold tile. The shadow spoke,
giving more shape and personality
to its presence. This presence had
a womanly voice, guiding me
into the farther corners of the
bathroom. Below my eyelids,
twins in their naked form,
like in a mother's womb,
were lying in a tub as if
it were a coffin.

In a somber tone, the mysterious
woman enlightened me, sharing
a tale about how to return
the twins to their rightful home.
According to her tale, the twins
were bound to hell unless we
orchestrated a ritual for their
souls to be released. By her
instruction, we proceeded to
the living room where my
vision tuned into the darkness.
Shafts of dim blue light casted
a glow around the mediocre
coffee table and sofa.

Two catholic nuns, draped in
stark black gowns, softly singing
old hymns, trailed in whilst
holding silver candelabras,
balancing three flickering, white
candlesticks. A few warm
bodies lied down on the floor
next to us as we clenched
dollar bills in our hands, close
to our chest. We were promised
a safe journey as long as we
gave the ferryman our money.
Gently, we closed our eyes
as the nuns wafted incense
over our faces. Gradually,
the nun's voices faded, as
a new vivid landscape
manifested before us.
There was a distant island,
covered in luscious green
forests and rocky mountains,
sitting on top of a vast ocean
with a blend of midnight blue
and teal waters. The wind carried
our spirits, floating from the high
skies till our toes kissed the ground.

A long line stretched beyond us,
along the sand-colored brick road,
trailing all the way to the double-
glass doors of an antique store.
Each of us lined ourselves
at the end, clinging to the money
we still held in our hands, wondering

which of the island dwellers were
the ferryman. Before I could free
myself from the tiresome line,
a young man dressed as a fox
hybrid revealed himself. He wore
emo-punk attire with a black shirt
titled 'Anime is my anti-drug'
and baggy, black pants with chains
and loose pockets. His hair was
as dark as his eyes and shaggy,
peeking out from under his
beanie that had holes
for his fox ears.

Leaning like a tilted tree
from a gust of wind, he closed
the gap between us, and whispered
into my ear, "Allow me to show you
something." Combing back my hair,
I prepared myself to follow him.
Walking side-by-side, we skipped
the long line and eased our way
into the antique room.
Like a chivalrous man, he swung
the door wide open for me,
waiting till I stepped through.
Beyond my expectations,
I was teleported in a jolting
fashion into a canoe.
It was as if all the age-old
decorations sitting on the
shelves were a mere illusion
that dispersed upon entry.

The trickster who tagged

me along rowed us across
the shimmering ocean.
"You do not belong here,"
he said in a distant, undertone
voice. I gazed at his broad back
and shifting shoulders, outlining
my vision of a gap shaped like he
between the tenacious trees
on the mountain-like island,
at the further edge of the shore.
Gliding along the sand, waves
guiding us safely to land, we stepped
off the canoe and planted our feet
on the sun-kissed ground.

An angel, from the peak
of the mountain island,
levitated down to the shore,
reuniting me with the twins
once more. Their hair as golden
yellow as sweet corn, running
to meet me with bare newborn skin,
white as milk, to return to the Earth again.

Death, Rebirth, Vampirism

Scrambling into the cave,
I witness its viscous jagged
rocks like those of alligator
teeth-the same teeth scraping
my head as I tumble foolishly.
Blood dripping and oozing like
milk from lactating breasts,
from the temple fountain
of my woozy skull. *Run! I must
escape this ghastly, ominous
tomb of endless tunnels.*

Clad in long, black robes
like a vampire from a Dracula
fairy tale, a chalky-skinned,
stalky figure motions towards me.
Traces of round cheeks
and a paper-thin jaw peer
from the dark shadows.
Horrendous, sharp nails reach
for my naked neck in sync with
a hissing sound of a striking snake.

Icy fangs pierce through
my skin to drain the life
source from a nutritious
vein of blood similar to
how a young cub sucks
from the mother's swollen,
milky-fruit. Fortune smiled

a wicked razor-toothed grin
at me, whilst sliding a wild-
licking tongue on the remnants
of my red velvet juice, dripping
from the puncture wounds,
deciding to spare my once
fragile, impermanent life
before the brink of death,
rapturing my pure silhouette
into oblivion.

A redeeming messenger
of sacred wisdom from
the depths of the veil
imparted with potent longing
unveiled the distant past
where him and I were once
in the astral realm as ancient
Vampiric lovers who lived for
thousands of years in unison,
settled in a lavish mansion.
Watchful eyes observed every
waking moment of my transition
like an owl with widened eyes
in the dead of night to keep its
baby chick in the line of sight.

Fangs curling down and
outward from buds to sharp
thorns. Nails stretching to
a pointed tip like claws
of a feline. Embracing the
newfound power for a brief
enriching moment till my
heightened Eagle sight captured

a gruesome display of my sister
bloodied and bare, dress torn
to shreds. Screeching fear
cemented on her face, mouth
agape, and soulless pupils.
The once angelic aura
glistening around her skin
was now snuffed out like
an abandoned match
that failed to light before
bursting into nothingness.

Blind rage bubbled inside me
like magma being violently
erupted from a long, stagnant,
mild slumber. Screams tore
out from the dark pits of my
throat, echoing sound ripples
for miles. The craving for
blood festered alongside
the extension of my Vampiric
claws, itching for the slaughter
of all my Vampiric brethren
whom I shared a likeness with
in powers, bestowed by the
quarter realms of the Underworld.

Swirls of blood hurled
and splattered maliciously,
painting the rough cave edges
blood red from one end of the
rocky-trail tunnels to the other.
Not a single Vampire was spared
my fierce wrath; claws and all
plunging through and ravaging
dead, stone-cold flesh. Baptizing

light sailed through the mouth
of the cave as I stood marked
by the blood-soaked white
dress. Clashing screams clung
for escape among the trees
for yards onward until they
could no longer resonate
from my sounding anguish.

Merciful Fangs

Cobblestone trails my pathway beneath Roman archways
teeming with robed pilgrims hustling to and fro.
A womanly figure approaches, appearing all alone.
Her eyes darted upward, casting dark shades
from the brim of her hood and its oversized frame.
Words sprang from her cracked, dry mouth, thirsting a soul
of youth from the waters of life to be revived tenfold.
Satisfying her request, I bit her neck with merciful fangs.
Unlike most vampires, my fangs were reserved for healing
the sick and withering souls. Fire of life flickered in her
eyes once more. Roman soldiers marched through with spears,
clearing the path, removing the healed woman, and stealing
her precious moment to bask in a rare, sacred power.

A middle pathway was forged amidst the sterling,
silver spears and thunderous stomping. I slipped through the
diverged crowd, evenly split into two. At the edge of town
I opened my palm like a budding flower to show
a black-lined tattoo symbol of a star to a bearded-Noah figure.
Tall of stature, and keen as a greyhound, he was
as he guarded the cave like a gatekeeper all alone.
Following the ways of Jesus, he broke bread with me.
He blessed the loaf I was about to devour, gifting
it with divine majestic powers yet to be whiffed
by a mere man. Solidified knowledge, manifested in lifting
yeast within the grain. One bite could transform my fate or risk
fracturing the entire balance society clung to. A delicate
line I stood on. I refused to hoard this knowledge
for myself and thus split the bread into smaller halves
and shared it with humanity. A wise man among the blanket
of frothy, white clouds invoked his wrath, calling

down lightning to strike the ground. Bursts of purple staffs
frenzied and rampaged around me. Thus was his rebuking.

Endangered Reptilians

Coarse sand grips my feet;
sand like Mars desert sand,
so dense and drying, it could
soak up water from the roots
of wheat. No wheat existed
or reigned on this desolate
plane. I walked forward
feeling drained while wearing
a plain, long, crimson robe.
Trailing a long path in the sand,
I was at last greeted by another
living organism at a secret
passageway of an underground
temple, dimly lit by concealed torches.

However, this living organism
was not of the same species.
This entity before me belonged
to the Reptilian race. Many who
were familiar with their kind
displaced them for being hostile,
malevolent creatures. I could not
negate its scaly, alligator-like skin,
yet, its hospitable welcome and
generous gestures betrayed the rumors
of maliciousness spun within webs
of myths around its kin. Down the
passageway, the Reptilian graciously
guided me, lighting the way with
the fire, from a torch, it gripped

tightly inside its inhuman hands-
shaped like dragon paws.

Past the hall, there was a curved
stone archway, leading as an
entrance to a sandstone platform,
surrounded by wide-rounded
pillars. Like giant humps of
a camel, sand mounds covered
the ground and the scenic background,
lit by more torches with corridor
entrances semi-blocked from the
deep sand. A few members of
the Reptilian clan sat around
the bare platform, synced with
the color of the surrounding sand.
They beckoned me forward
to sit and listen.

One amongst them, an elder
claimed to have descended
from a long line of Reptilian
peacemakers who were esteemed
as benevolent lizards among
the Egyptians, living in coexistence,
and aiding the planet. They were
once again requesting assistance
to continue their mission of helping
the planet heal; to be restored, like
centuries long before. However, for
many years, they were warned of
their extinction. Now, a dying race,
they were faced with a dire
circumstance, and an important
decision to make. The three elder

Reptilians, sitting so peacefully,
prayed and pleaded, seeking my help.

Inconceivable it was to believe
I was their ultimate savior.
I merely saw myself as an
observer. Helplessness weighed
on me like a thousand bricks
piled on my back by all my
ancestors in Heaven. Oxygen
was mechanically driven and
filtered through a metal brace
encasing the tiny frame
of the Reptilian infant's rib
cage. With premature wings
like that of a bat, it flew towards
me as it strived to breathe through
the machine. Hopelessness tugged
at my heartstrings. Not even the
machine could save its kind.

My heart and mind
pitied what was left
of the poor thing,
at the end of its line.
Down the family tree,
oxygen could not be
easily filtered through
the lungs from the deviation
in the atmosphere. Moist,
green grass softened my
seat in front of the newborn
Reptilian whose machine
continued pumping for air
until it was no longer……

…………..breathing.

First a Heroine Then a Bride

Darkest blue, oh oceans of Divine
Mother where I seek my truth.
My dainty, pale body collapses
into your watery womb. Where
sea foam clashes with my skin
and tissue. I sink further down
with the white frills of my gown,
swishing around. Fish shaped like
women, born of unrivaled beauty,
stretched their arms forth to capture
me whilst I was sinking. These
Sirens swam with great agility,
using their fins as they carried me
with them. We drifted and drifted
beyond any sea or ocean that dwelled
within the waters familiar to me.

Of what world have I been
stranded upon that exists across
space, millions of light years away?
An aquatic dream, made of pure
water, a habitat for amphibians.
Here I am curled in a ball, floating
in the embracing waters of this
unknown planet. My captor, Sirens
speak to me, giving a decree to save
the dying creatures. For only then will
they set me free. Time on Earth flowed
differently for my father, who searched
endlessly to find me. His sanity endured

a brutal reality--one where his daughter
was not to be seen. He thought about
ending his life after so many years
had passed, thinking it could be easy
to fall from a cliffside to be claimed,
body and soul, by the sea.

All hope was lost until, finally,
I returned gracefully. My mission
on the aquatic planet was complete,
allowing the Sirens to release me.
I was tightly gripped by my father's
embrace. It was as if he feared
the tiniest gust of wind would
whisk me away. After releasing me,
he shined a green laser from a little
light device to spot a suitable husband
to court me and marry into the family.
As the green light scanned across
the bleachers of the giant stadium,
my gifted foresight allowed me
to perceive the truth of a man's
entire identity and lifespan within
a flash. At the pointed direction
of my father's green light device,
there was a man I judged to be
a suitable match.

Unto Death, We Become One

Visage of ancient wisdom
Wrapped around immortal
Bones paired with skin and
Hair of ash but a soul drunk
On love sweetened like the
Blooming of cherry blossoms

Wandering eyes of a Death
God vessels of sight that
Hath seen beyond the
Worldly light witnessing
Ugly decay and the beauty
Of life living, breathing, and
Dying in the wake of his
Judgement in one big swirl
Of Universal cycles

In the darkest pit
My bare body glowed
A whiteness like pure
Snow the Death God
Lowered his head to
Reach me from down
Below with an unknown
Yearning he marked me
With his soft lips
Determining my life
Unworthy of being
Forfeit, instead he
Desired nothing more
Than to be merged
With me as one body
For eternity